The big wet balloon

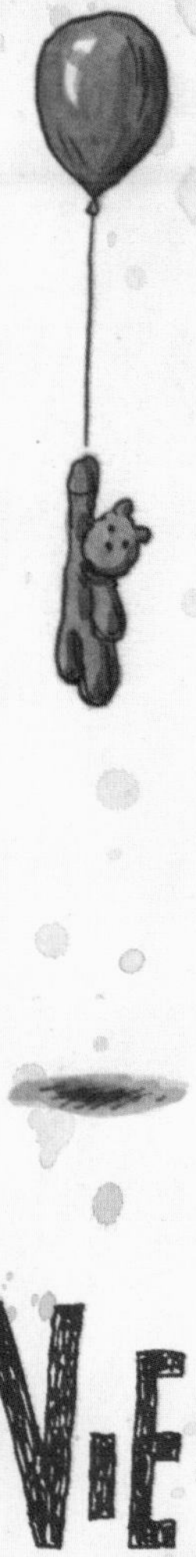

Liniers

THE
BIG WET
BALLOON

A TOON BOOK BY

LINIERS

TOON BOOKS · NEW YORK

PARENTS MAGAZINE 10 BEST CHILDREN'S BOOKS 2013
2014 EISNER AWARD NOMINEE
ALA GRAPHIC NOVEL READING LIST 2014

For Matilda and Clementina...my little muses

Editorial Director: FRANÇOISE MOULY

Book Design: FRANÇOISE MOULY & RICARDO LINIERS SIRI

LINIERS' artwork was done using ink, watercolor, and drops of rain.

A TOON Book™ © 2013 Ricardo Liniers & TOON Books, an imprint of RAW Junior, LLC, 27 Greene Street, New York, NY 10013. No part of this book may be used or reproduced in any manner whatsoever without written permission except in the case of brief quotations embodied in critical articles and reviews. TOON Graphics™, TOON Books®, LITTLE LIT® and TOON Into Reading!™ are trademarks of RAW Junior, LLC. All rights reserved. All our books are Smyth Sewn (the highest library-quality binding available) and printed with soy-based inks on acid-free, woodfree paper harvested from responsible sources. Printed in Malaysia by Tien Wah Press. Distributed to the trade by Consortium Book Sales; orders (800) 283-3572; orderentry@perseusbooks.com; www.cbsd.com.

Library of Congress Cataloging-in-Publication Data: Liniers, 1973- The big wet balloon : a TOON book / by Liniers. pages cm. – (Easy-to-read comics. Level 2) Summary: "Matilda promises her little sister Clemmie an amazing weekend spent playing outside. But the weather's rainy and Clemmie can't bring her new balloon along. Matilda teaches Clemmie all the delights of a wet Saturday"– Provided by publisher. ISBN 978-1-935179-32-0 (alk. paper) 1. Graphic novels. [1. Graphic novels. 2. Sisters–Fiction. 3. Rain and rainfall–Fiction. 4. Balloons–Fiction.] I. Title. PZ7.7.L56Bi 2013 741.5'973–dc23 2012047662

ISBN: 978-1-935179-32-0

15 16 17 18 19 20 TWP 10 9 8 7 6 5 4 3

WWW.TOON-BOOKS.COM

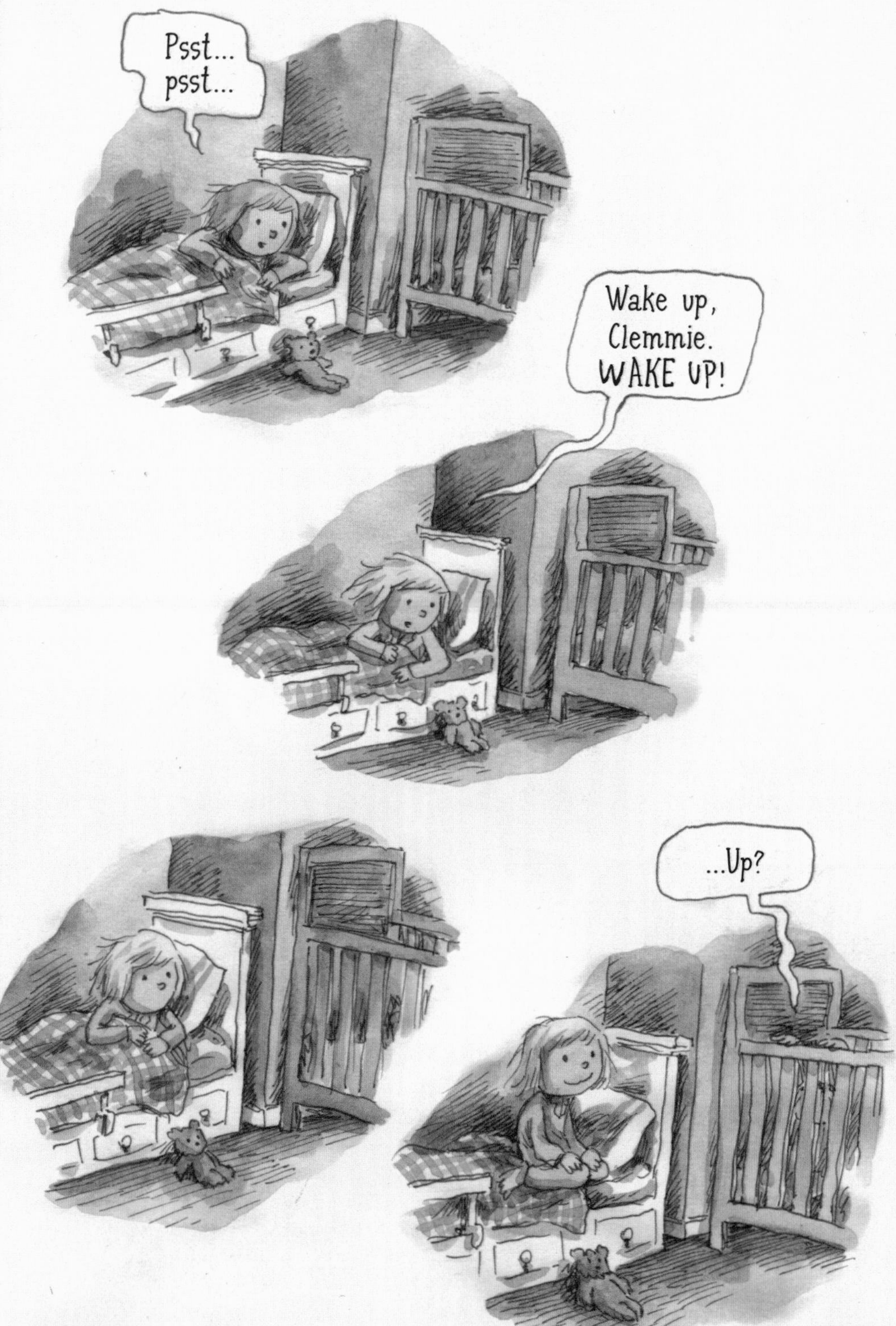
Psst...
psst...
Wake up,
Clemmie.
WAKE UP!
...Up?

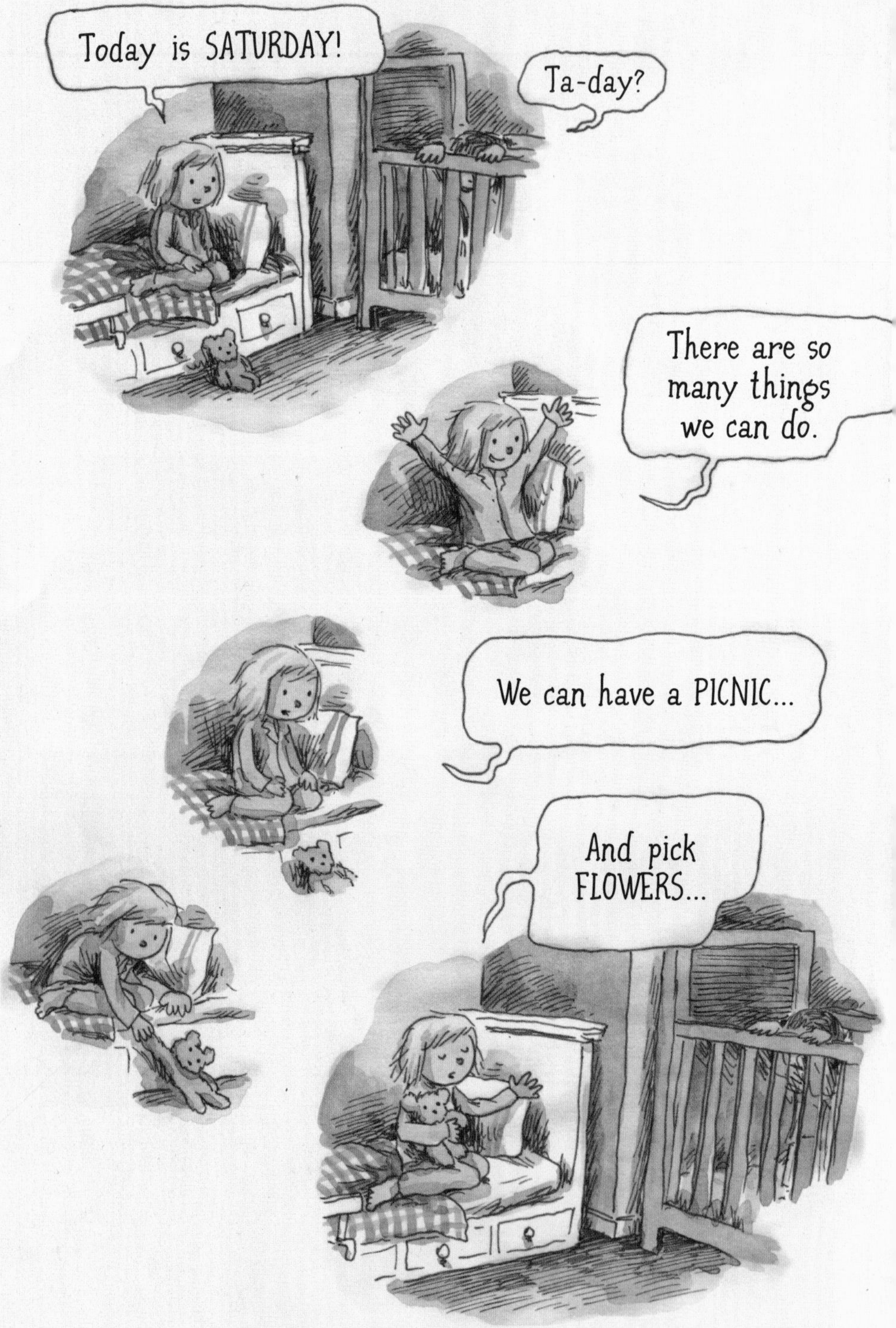
Today is SATURDAY!
Ta-day?
There are so many things we can do.
We can have a PICNIC...
And pick FLOWERS...

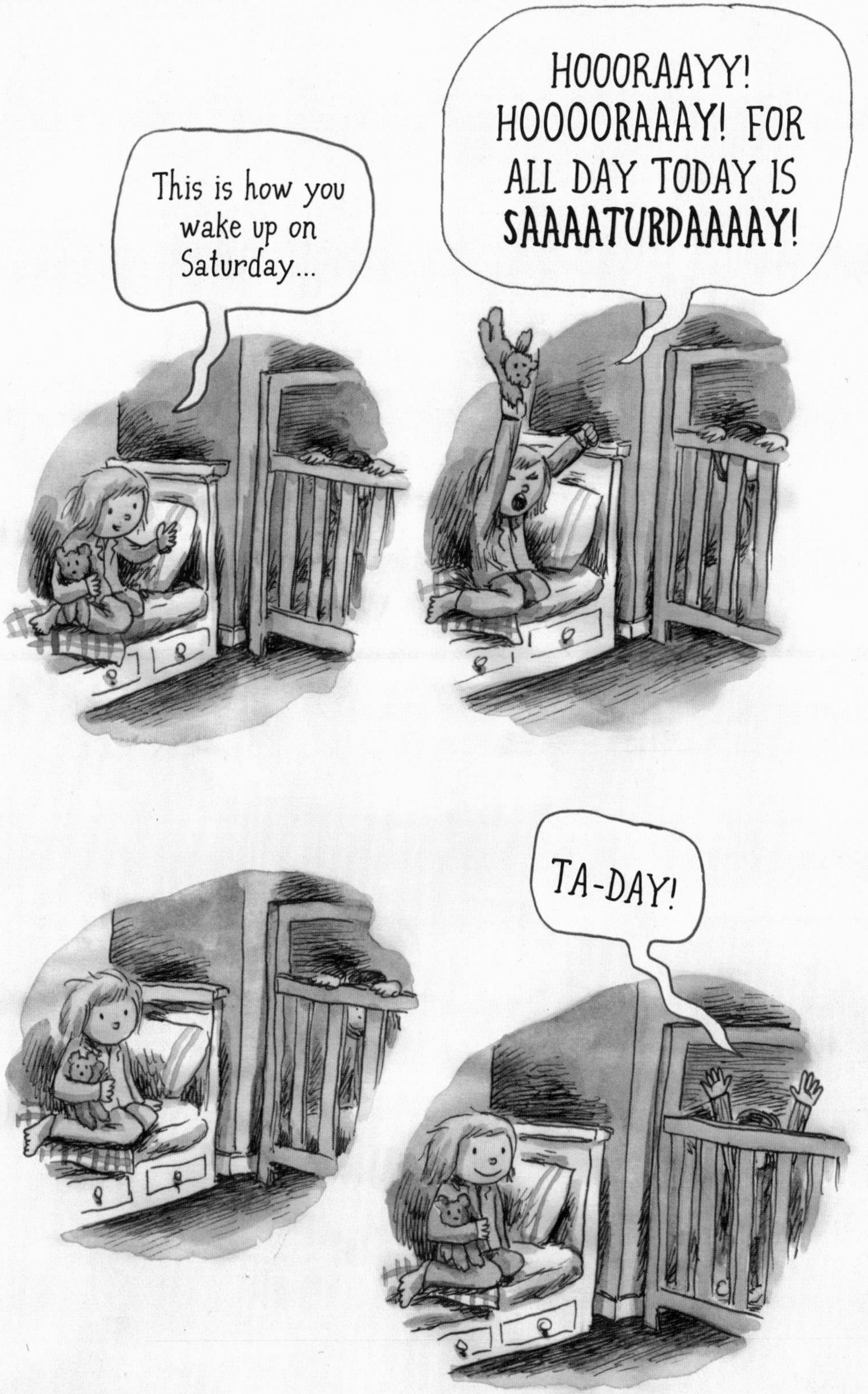
This is how you wake up on Saturday...
HOOORAAYY! HOOOORAAAY! FOR ALL DAY TODAY IS SAAAATURDAAAAY!
TA-DAY!

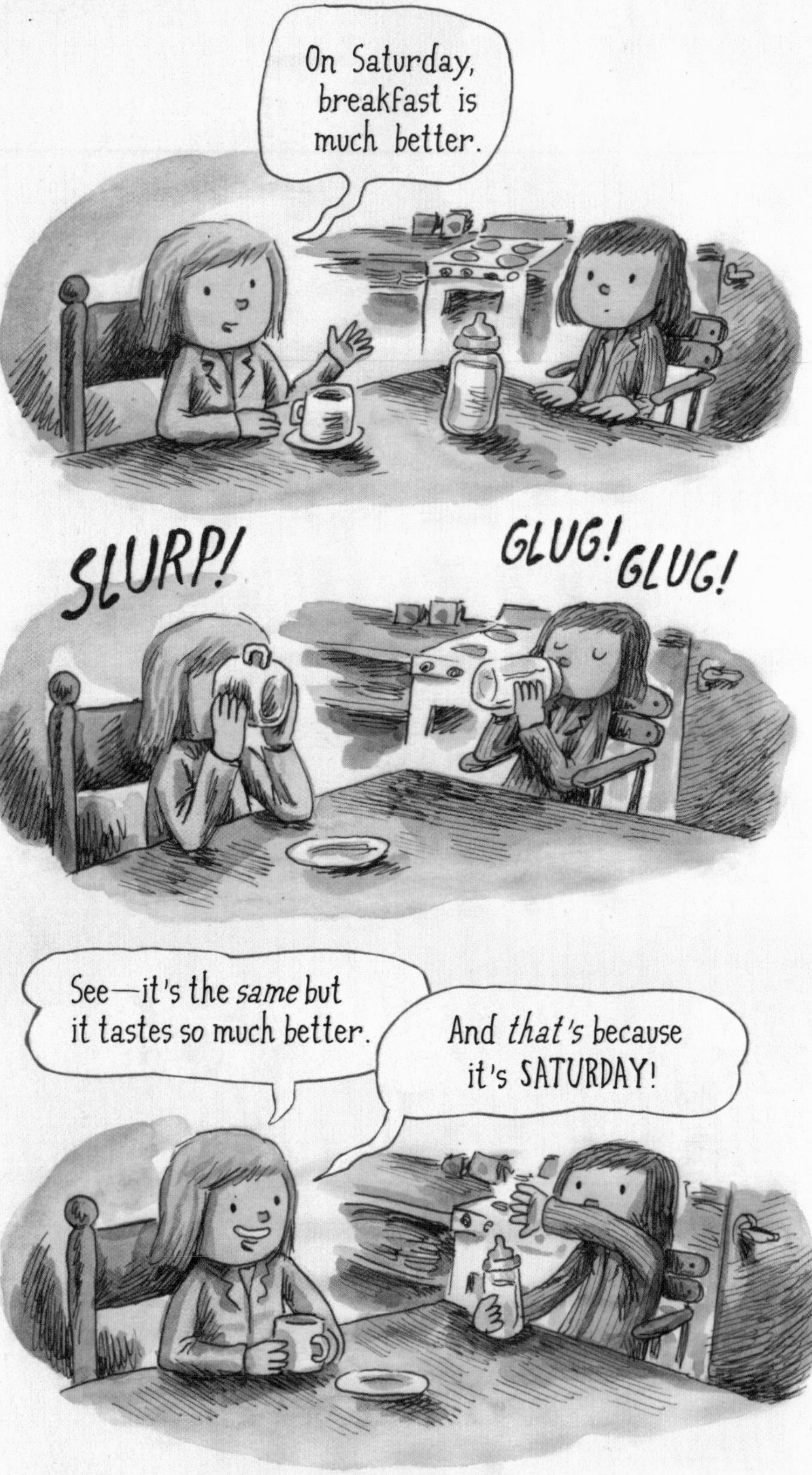
On Saturday, breakfast is much better.
SLURP!
GLUG! GLUG!
See—it's the *same* but it tastes so much better.
And *that's* because it's SATURDAY!

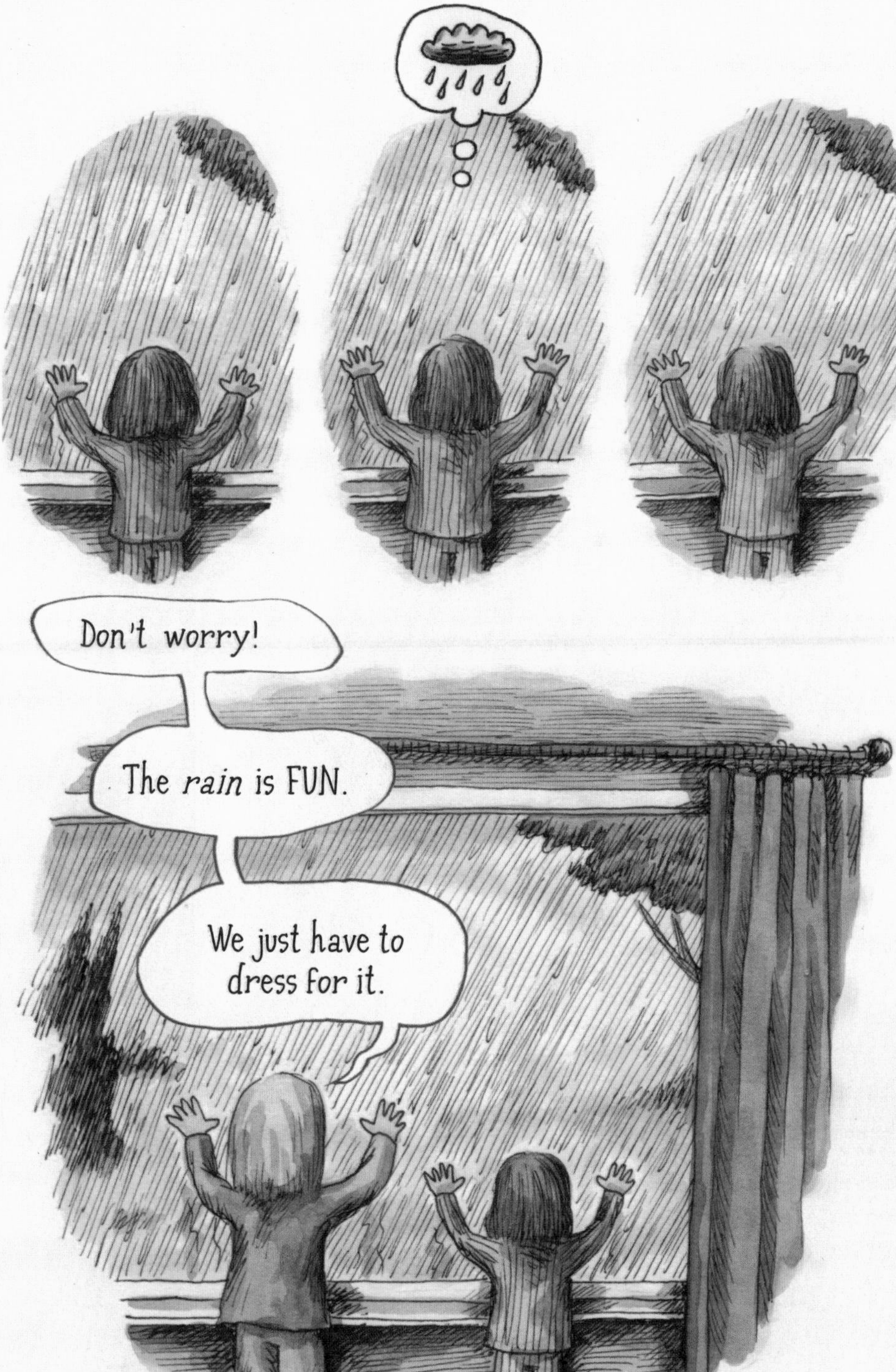

Don't worry!
The *rain* is FUN.
We just have to dress for it.

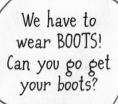
We have to
wear BOOTS!
Can you go get
your boots?

Ha ha! That's
not your *BOOTS!*

That's the red
BALLOON from
your birthday!

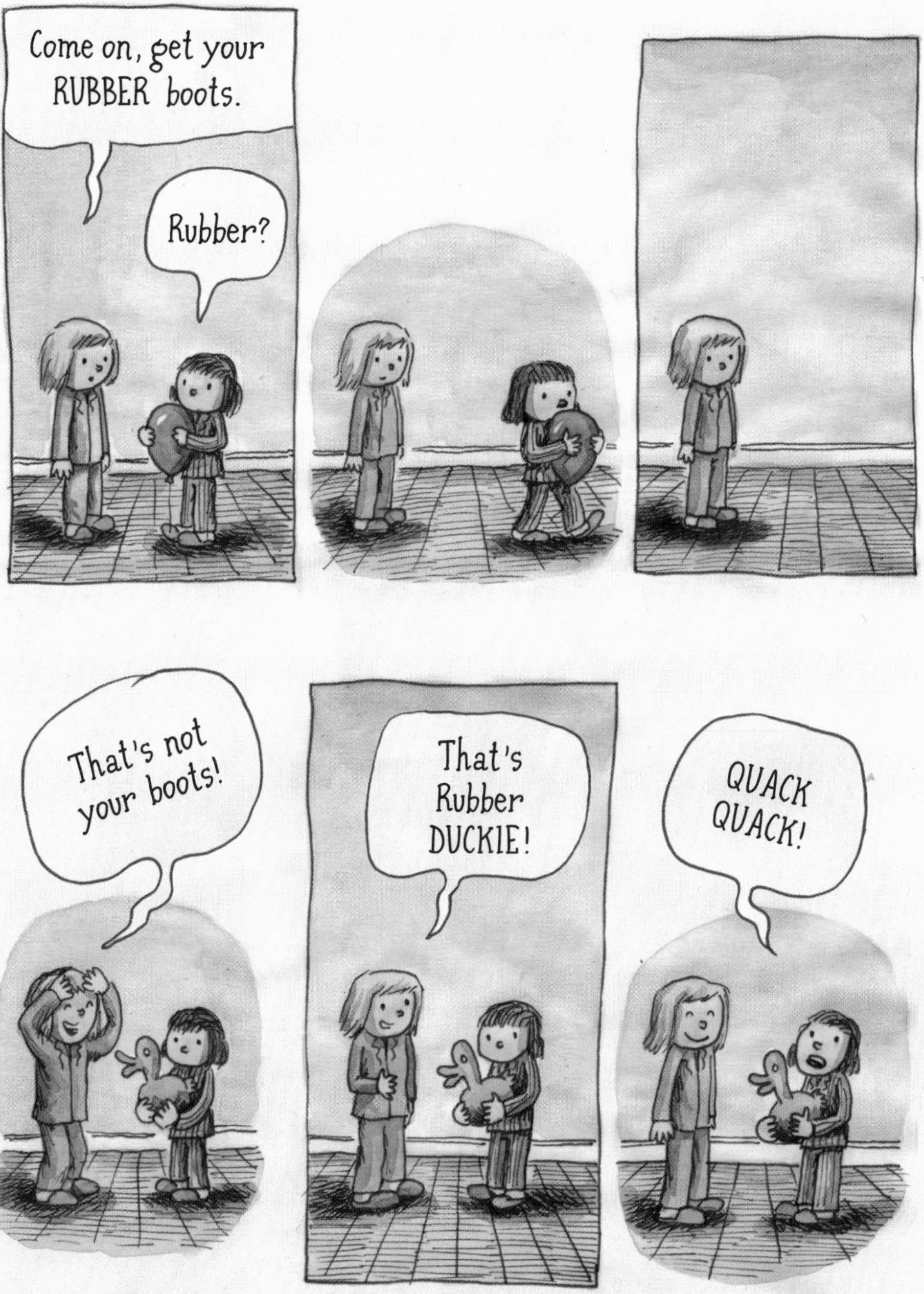
Come on, get your RUBBER boots.
Rubber?
That's not your boots!
That's Rubber DUCKIE!
QUACK QUACK!

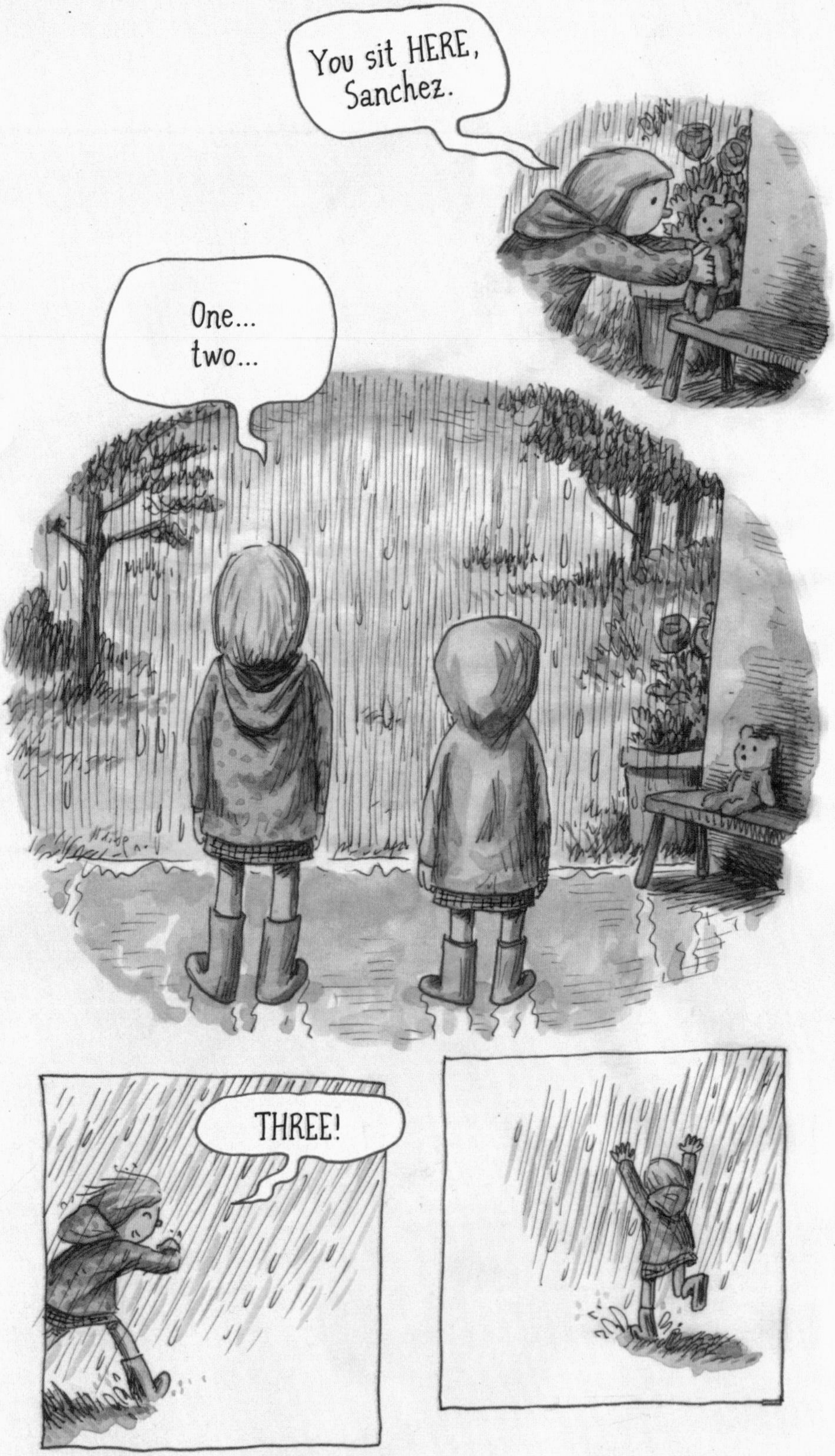
You sit HERE, Sanchez.
One... two...
THREE!

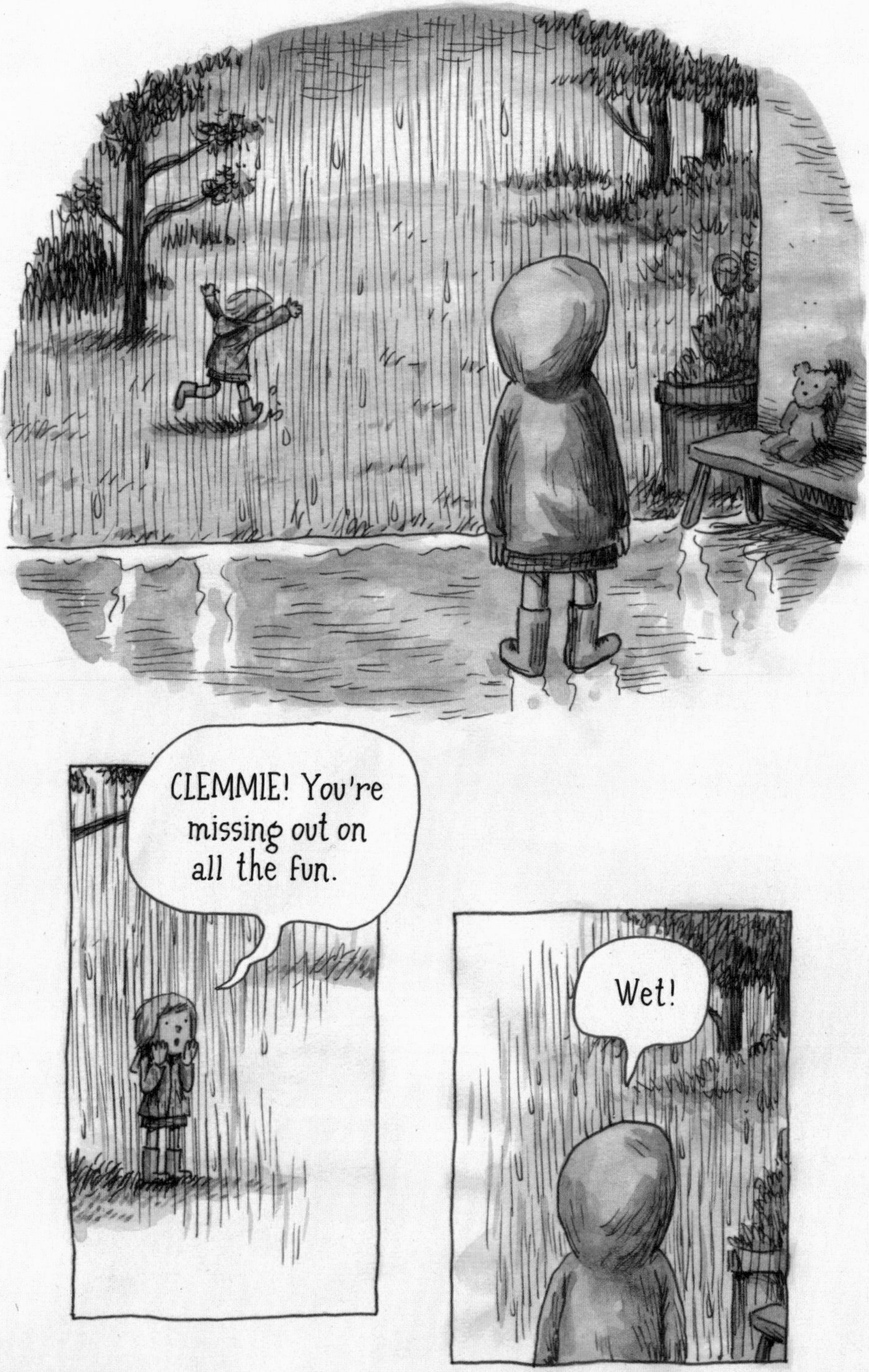
CLEMMIE! You're missing out on all the fun.
Wet!

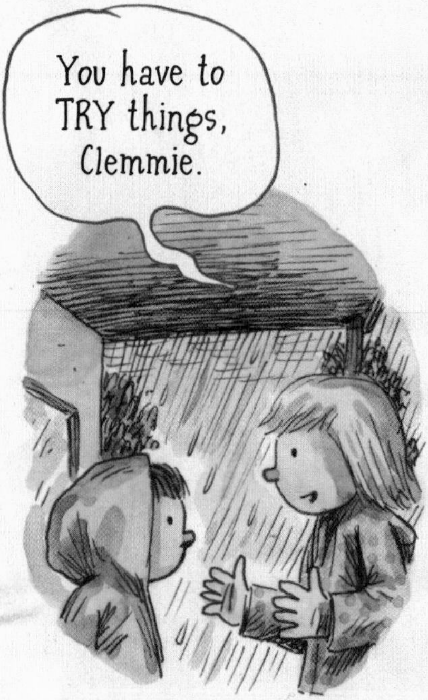
You have to TRY things, Clemmie.

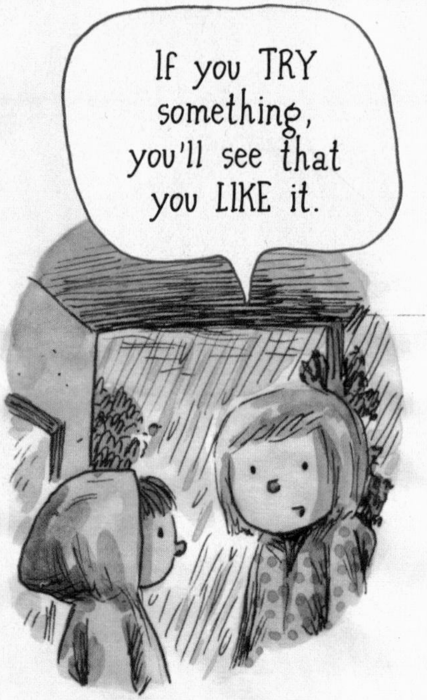
If you TRY something, you'll see that you LIKE it.

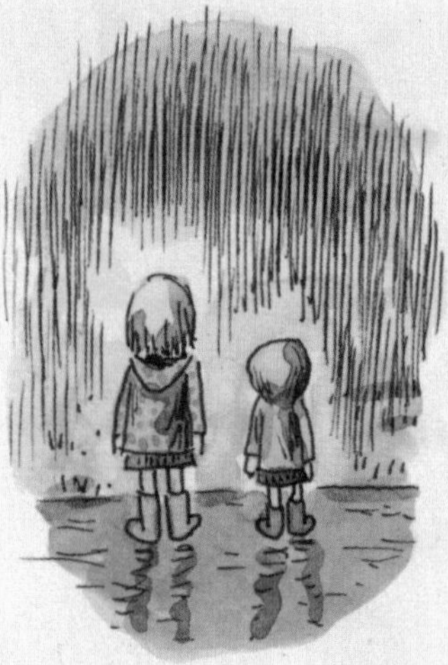

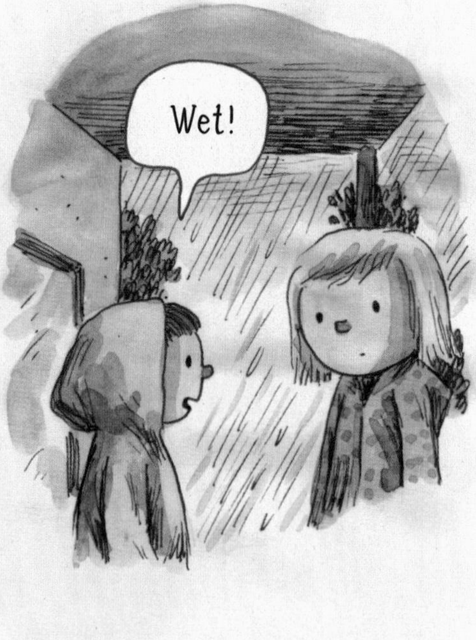
Wet!

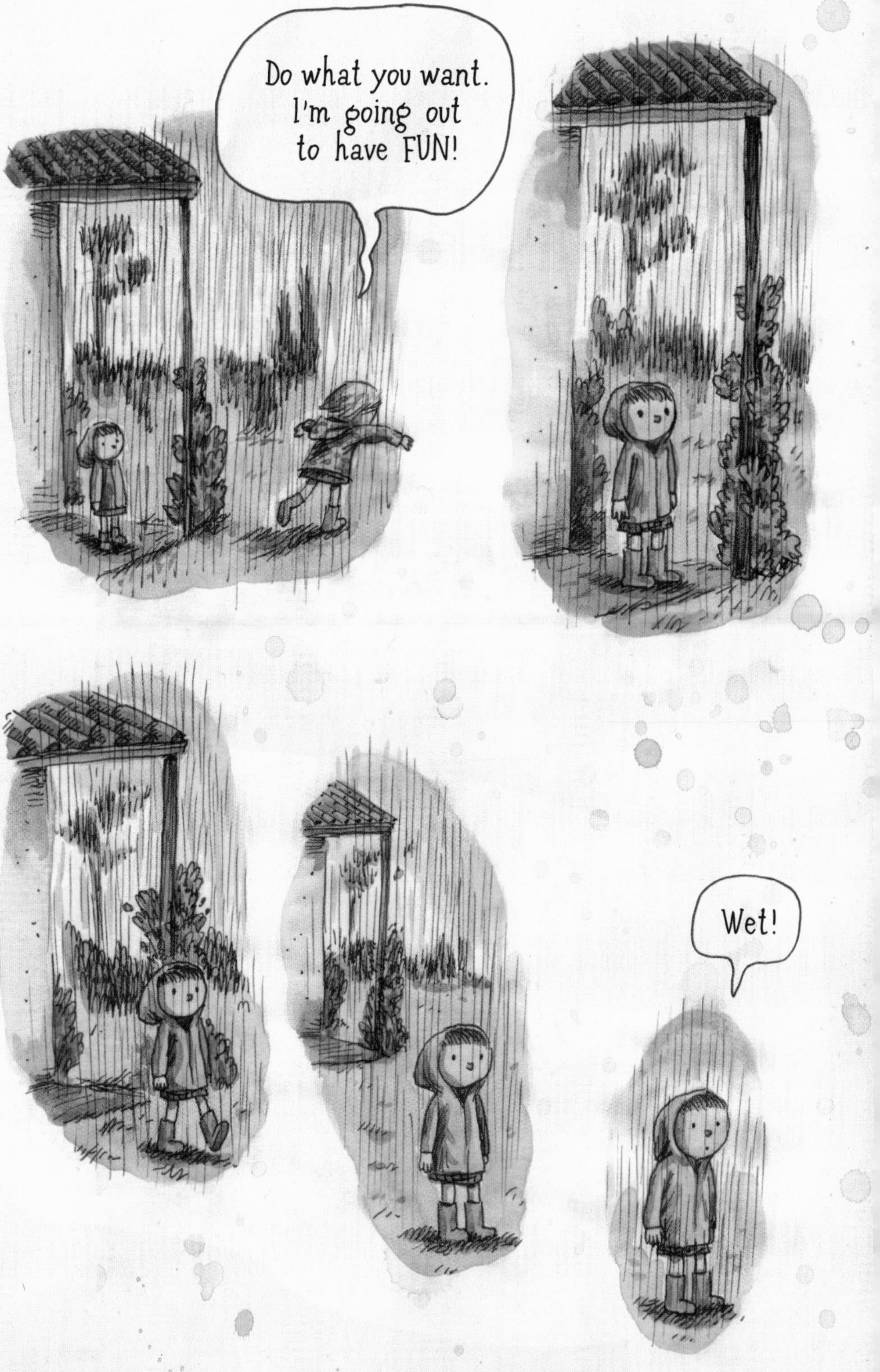
Do what you want. I'm going out to have FUN!
Wet!

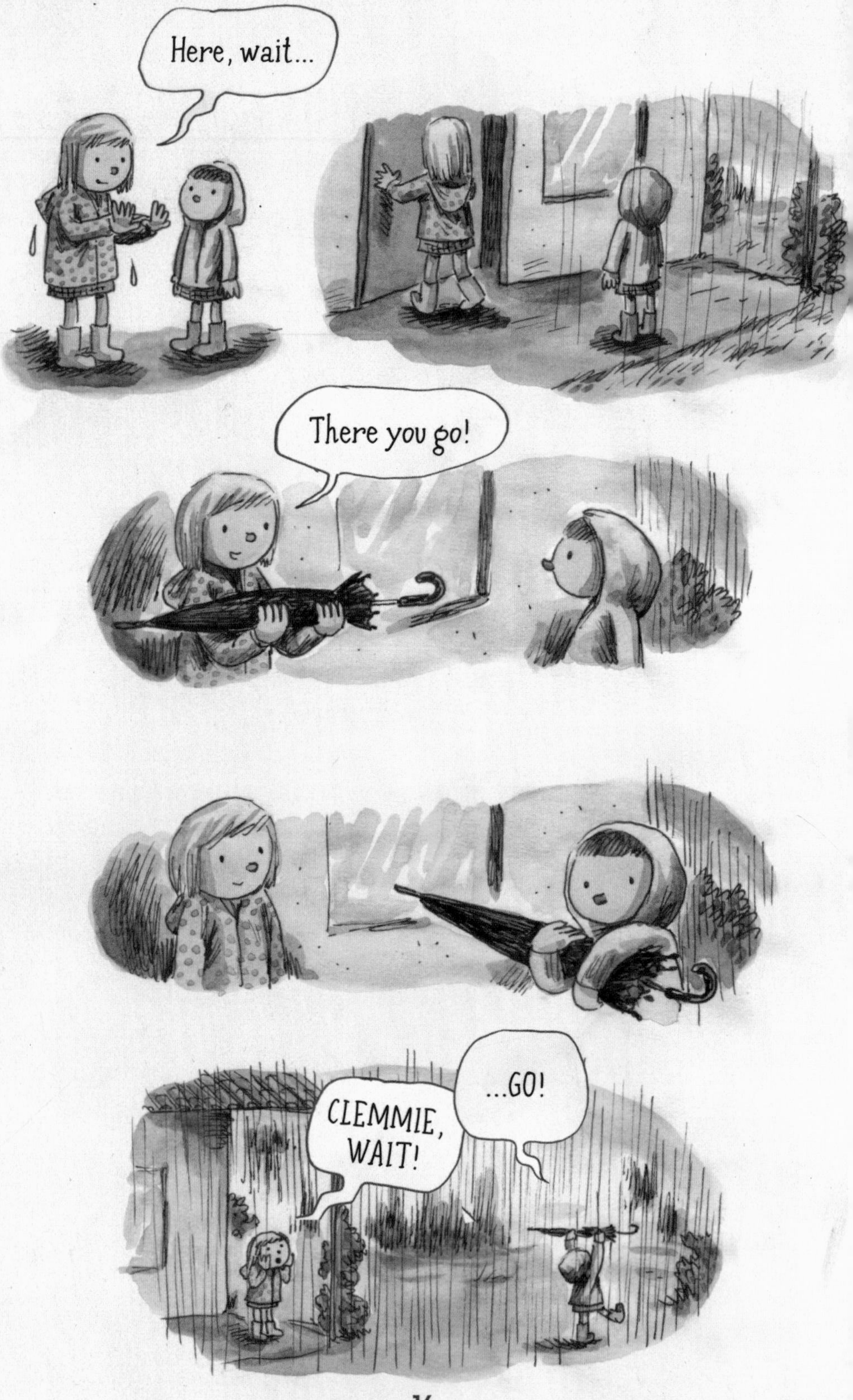
Here, wait...
There you go!
CLEMMIE, WAIT!
...GO!

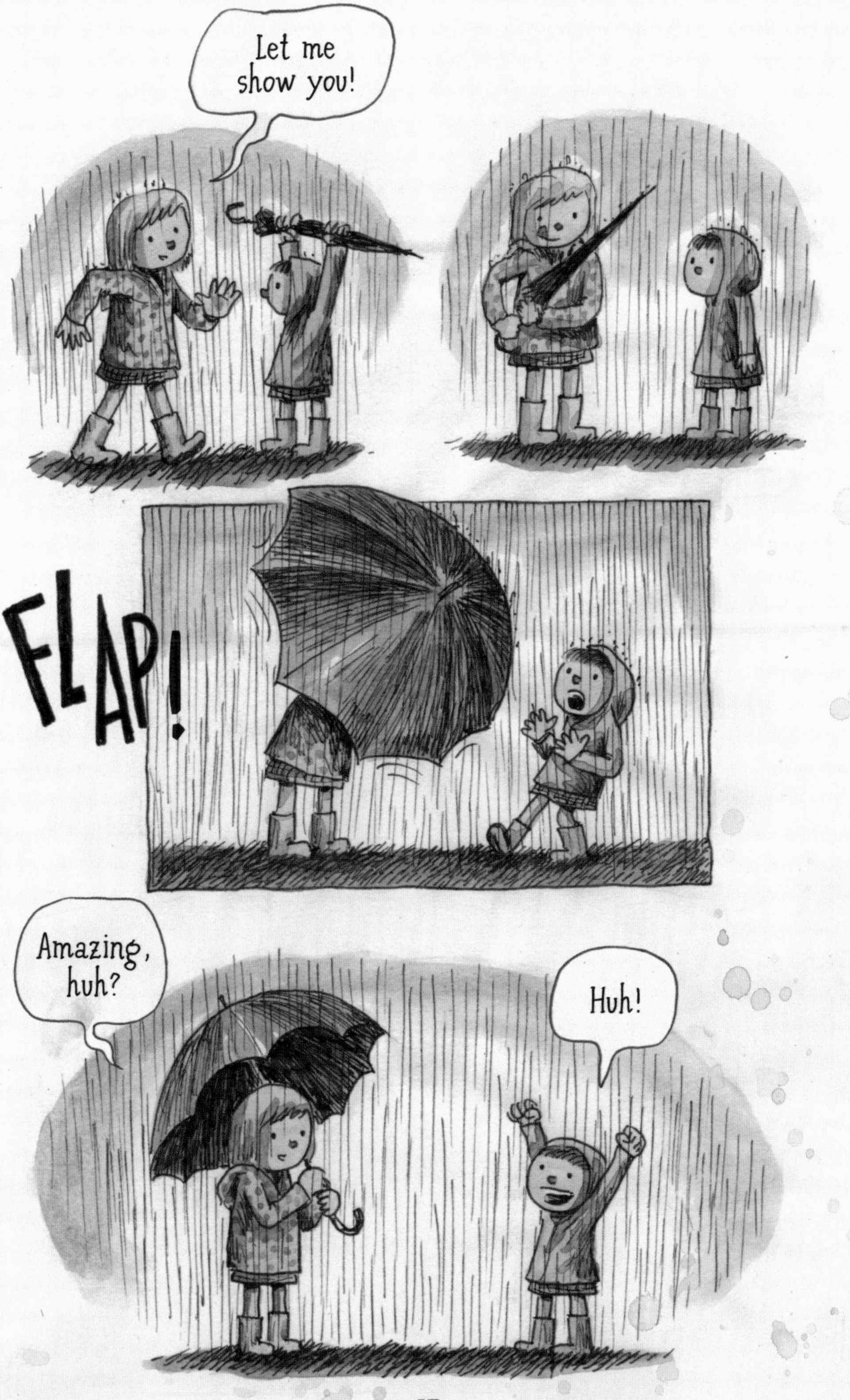
Let me show you!
FLAP!
Amazing, huh?
Huh!

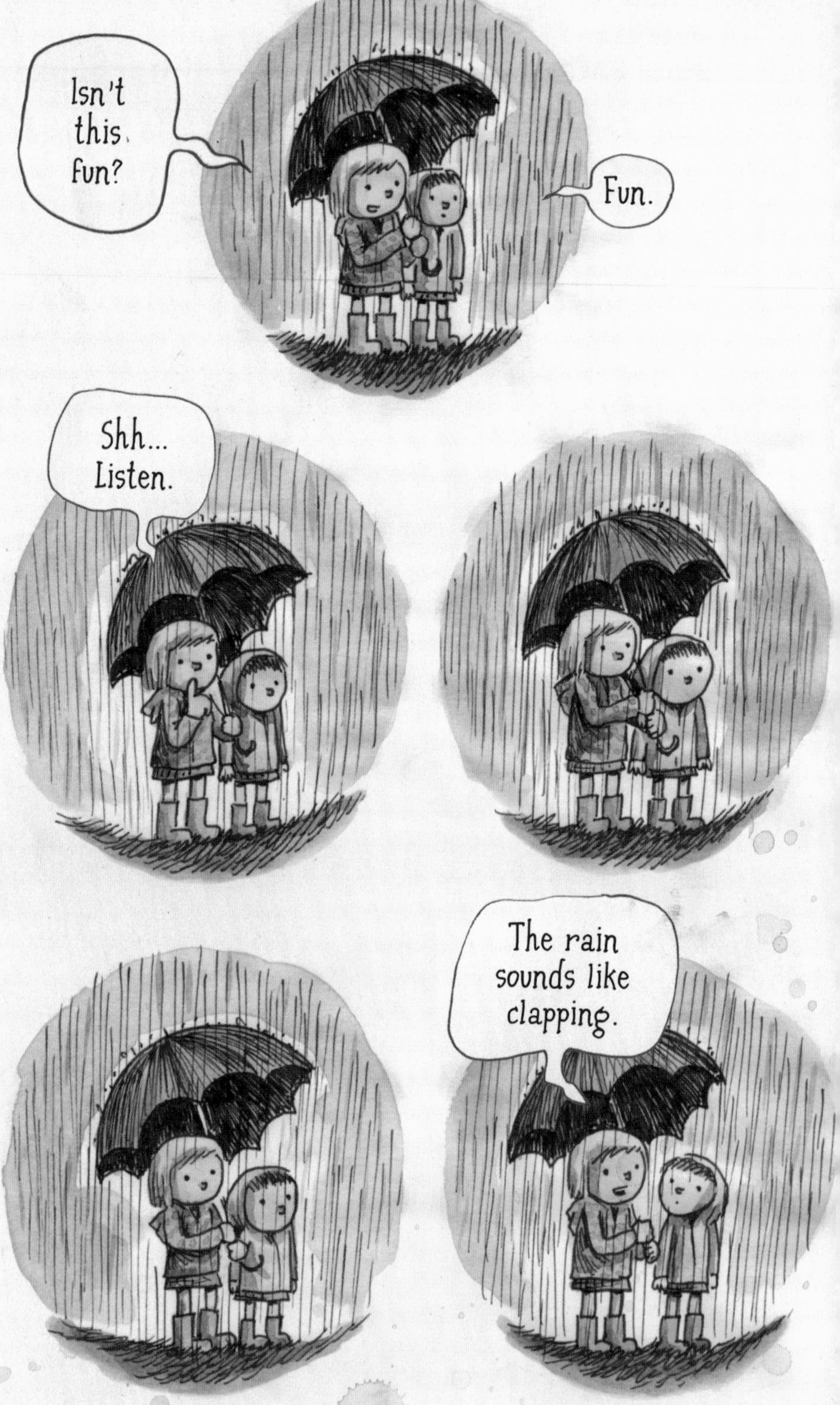
Isn't this fun?
Fun.
Shh... Listen.
The rain sounds like clapping.

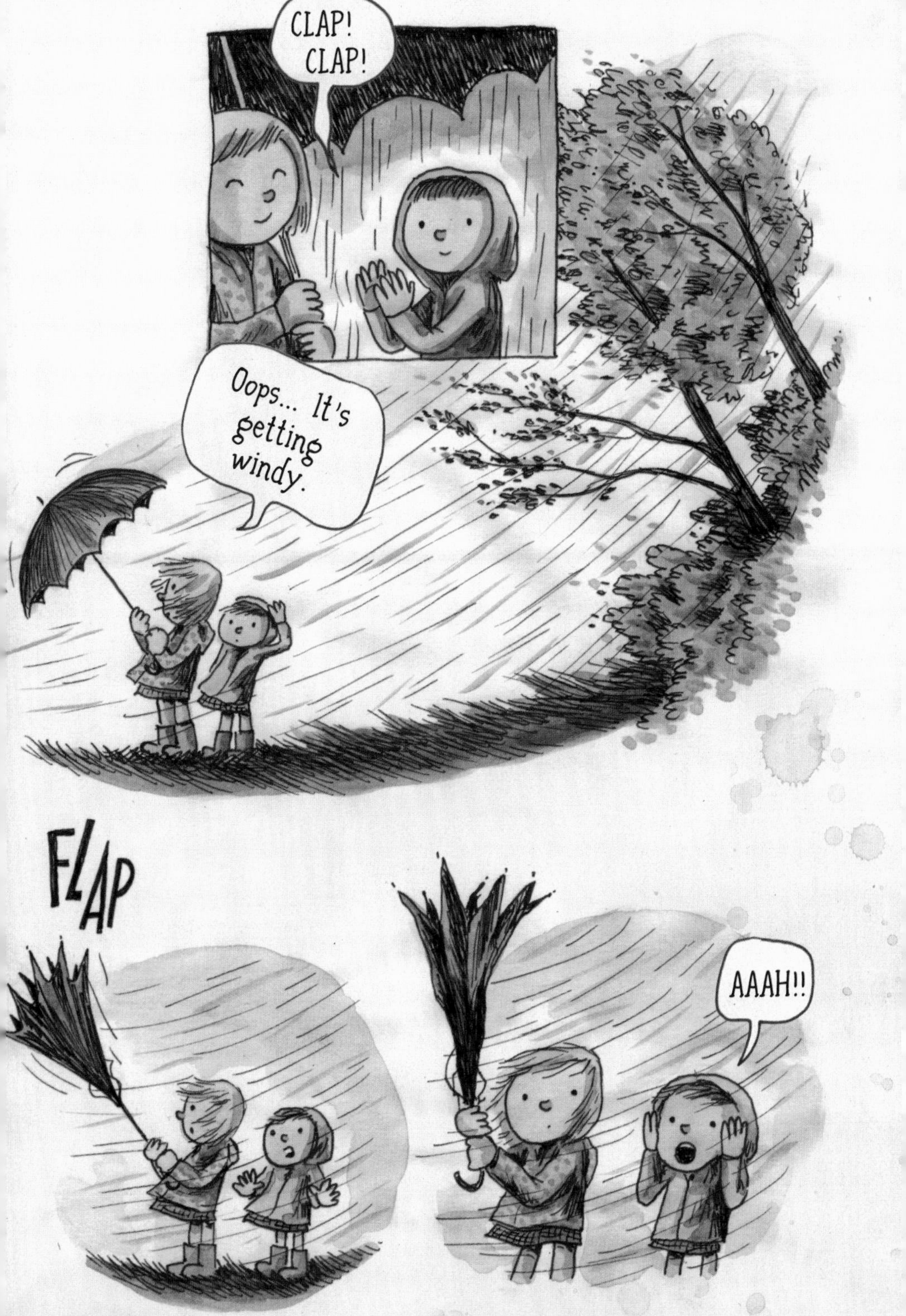
CLAP! CLAP!
Oops... It's getting windy.
FLAP
AAAH!!

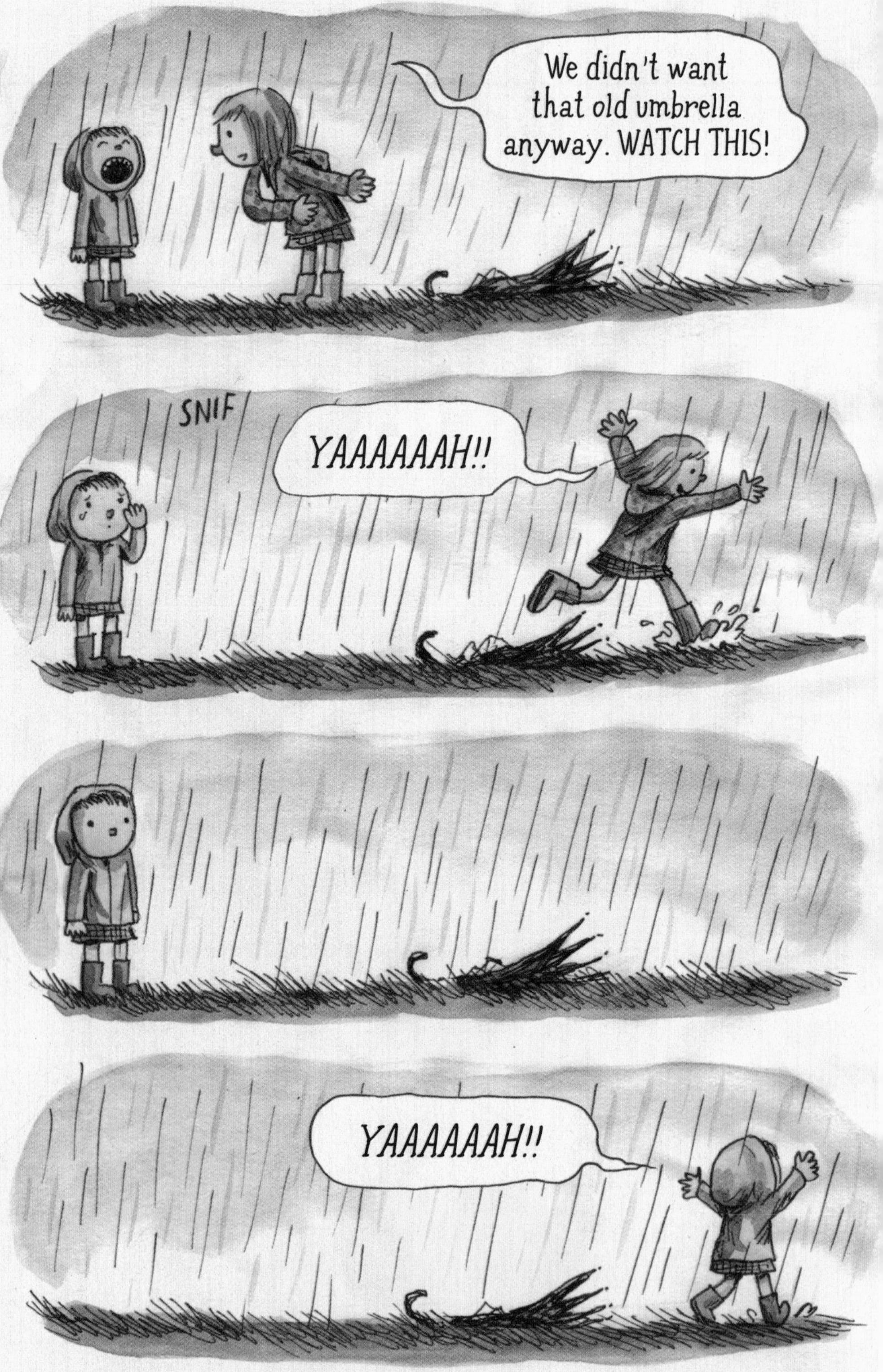
We didn't want that old umbrella anyway. WATCH THIS!
SNIF
YAAAAAAH!!
YAAAAAAH!!

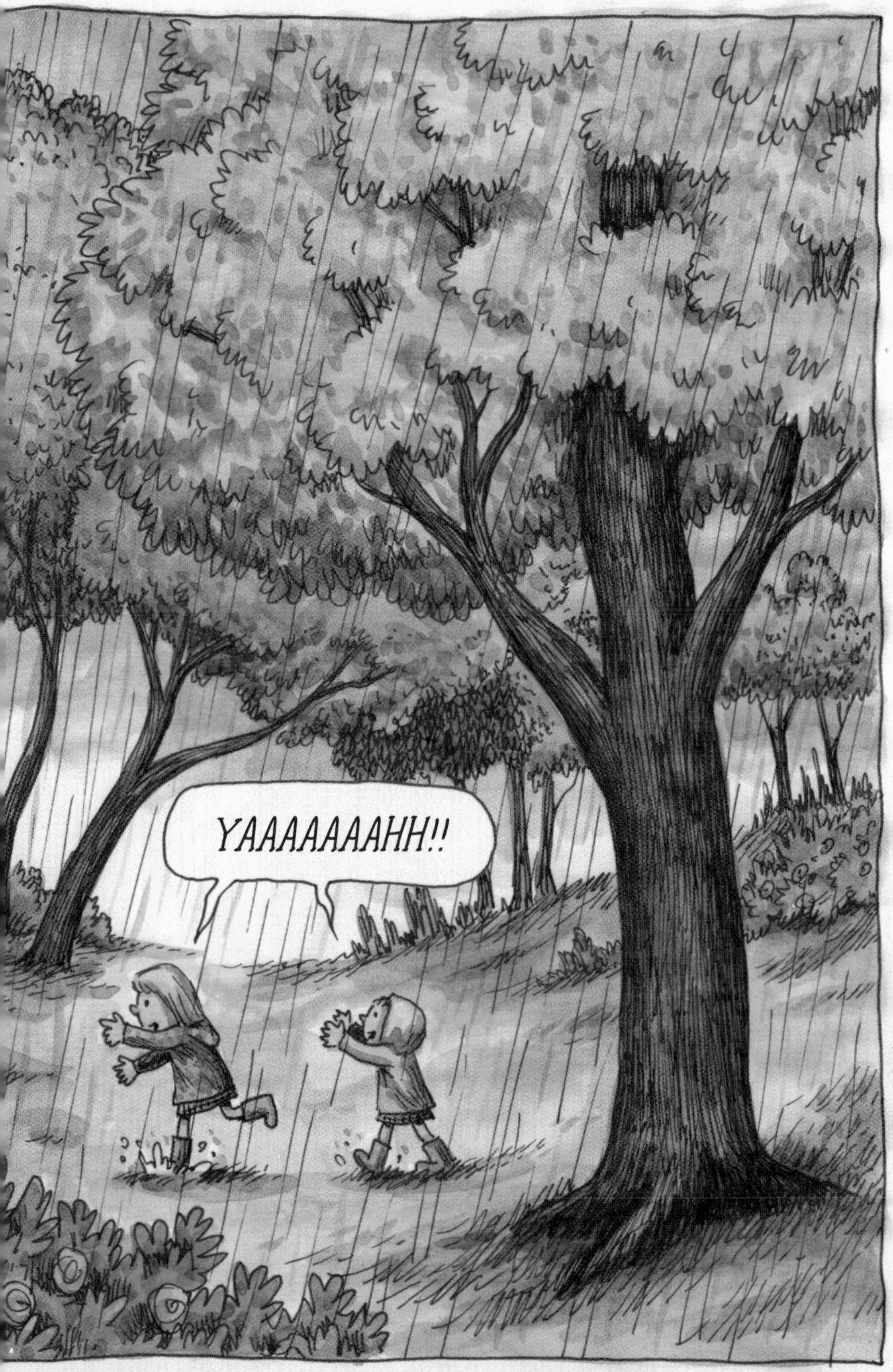
YAAAAAAAHH!!

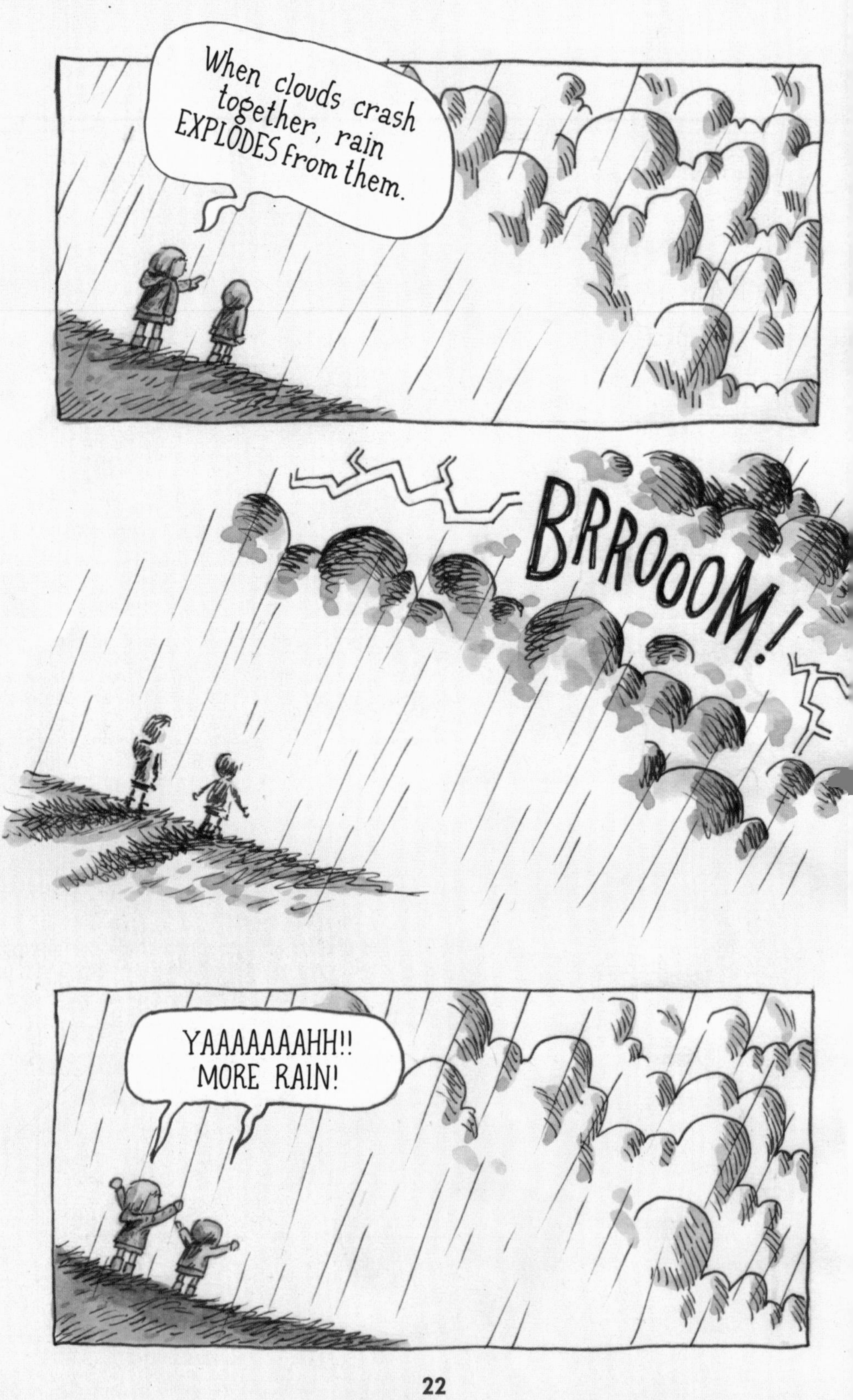
When clouds crash together, rain EXPLODES from them.
BRROOOM!
YAAAAAAAHH!! MORE RAIN!

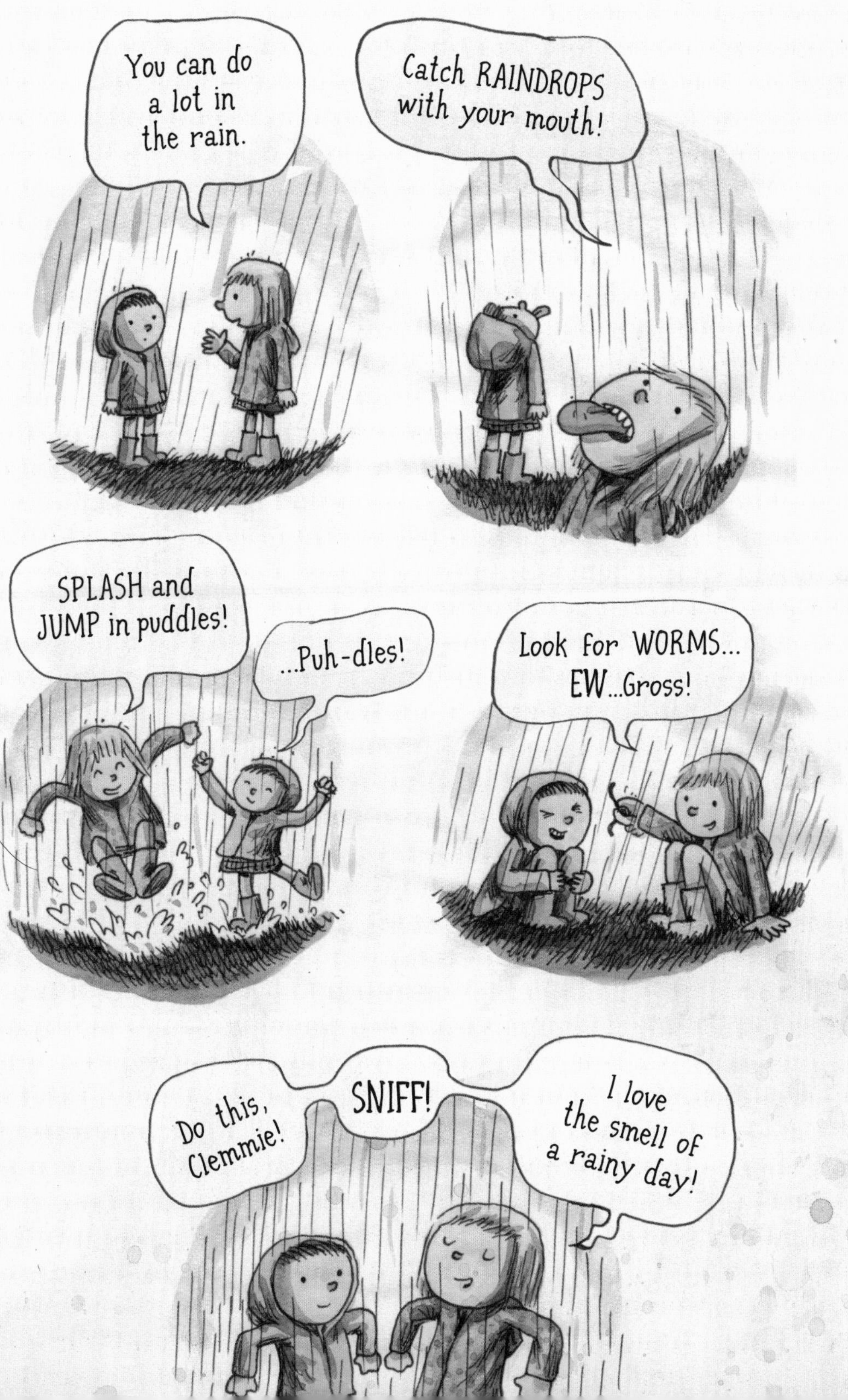
You can do a lot in the rain.
Catch RAINDROPS with your mouth!
SPLASH and JUMP in puddles!
...Puh-dles!
Look for WORMS... EW...Gross!
Do this, Clemmie!
SNIFF!
I love the smell of a rainy day!

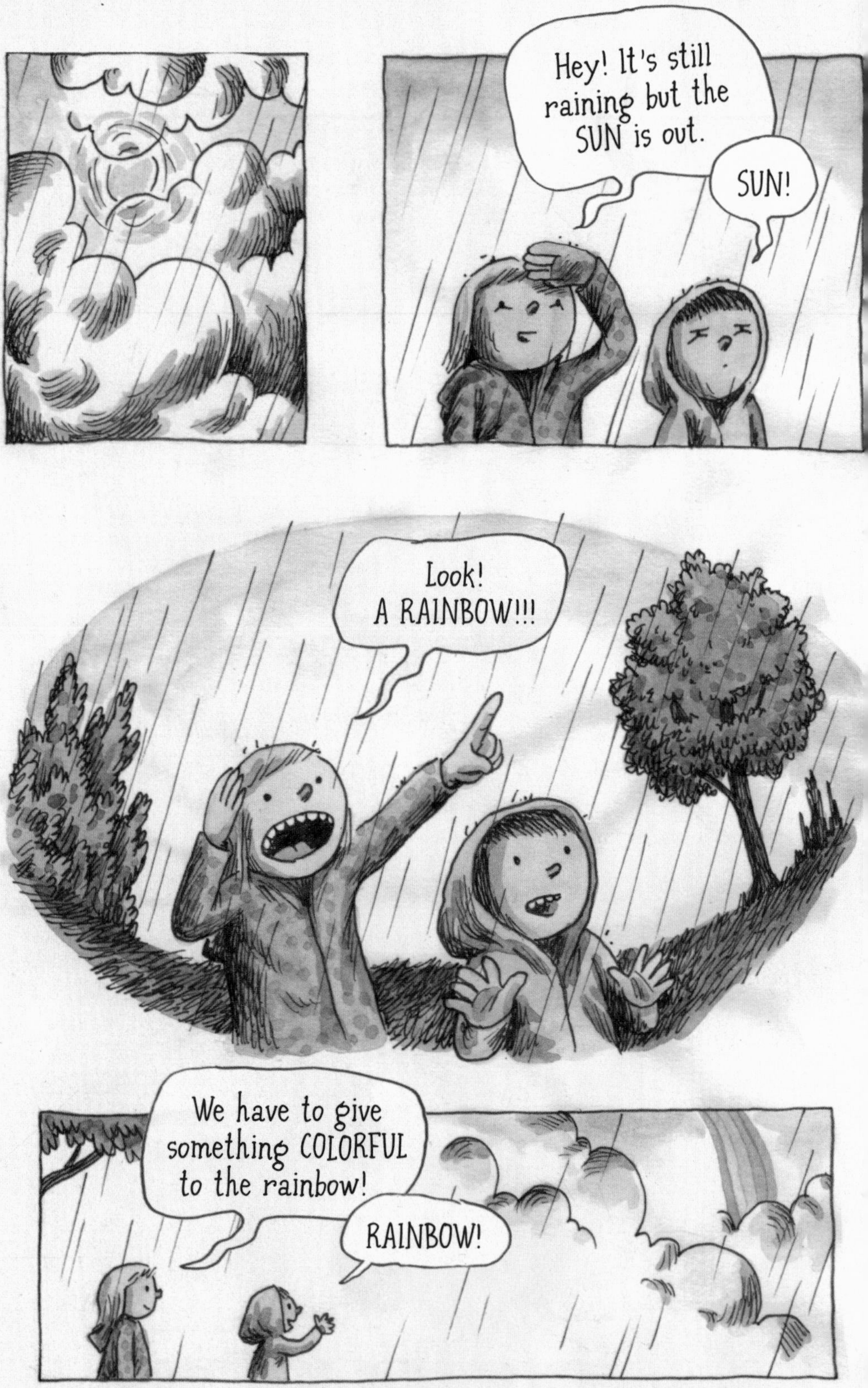
Hey! It's still raining but the SUN is out.
SUN!
Look! A RAINBOW!!!
We have to give something COLORFUL to the rainbow!
RAINBOW!

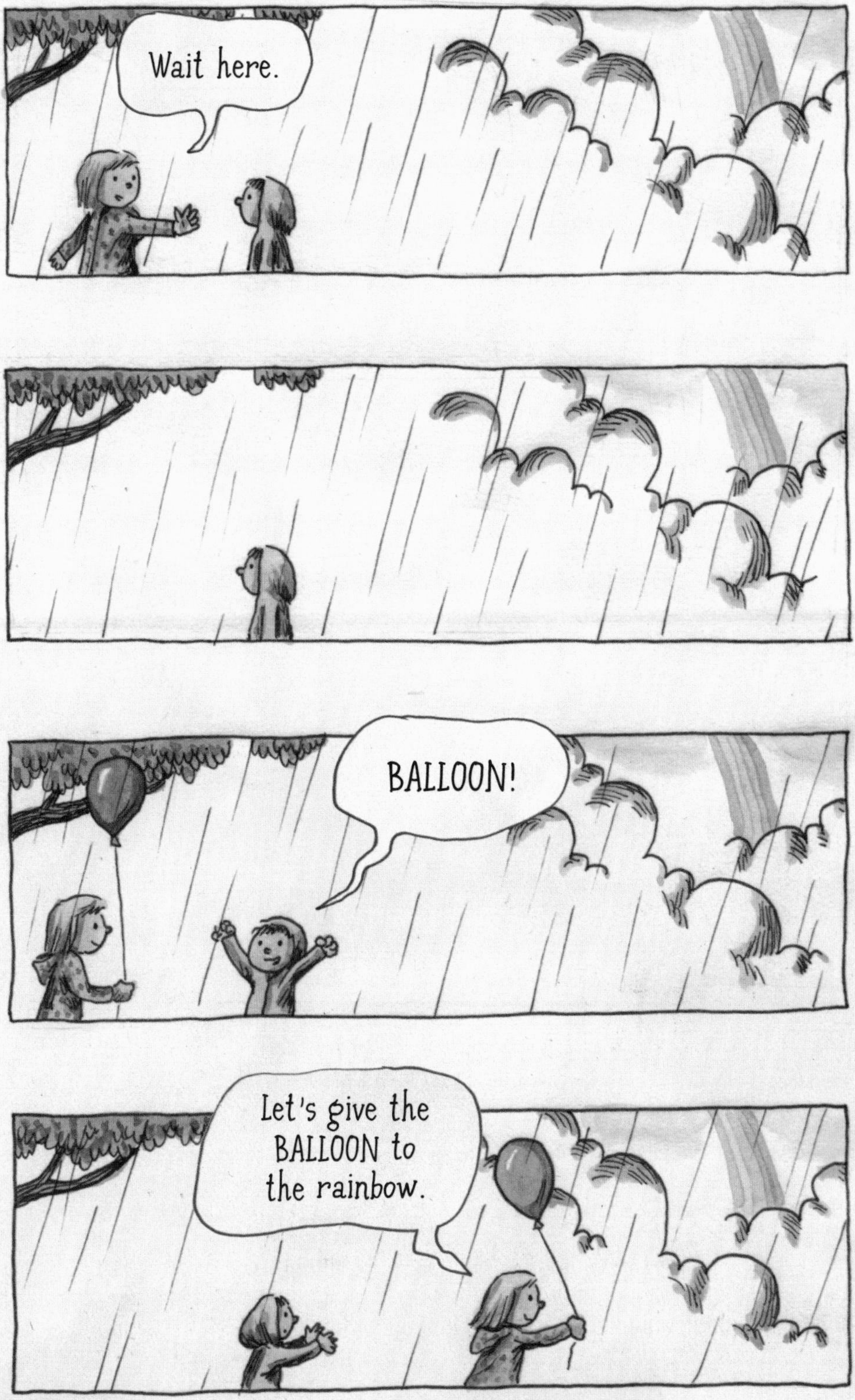
Wait here.
BALLOON!
Let's give the BALLOON to the rainbow.

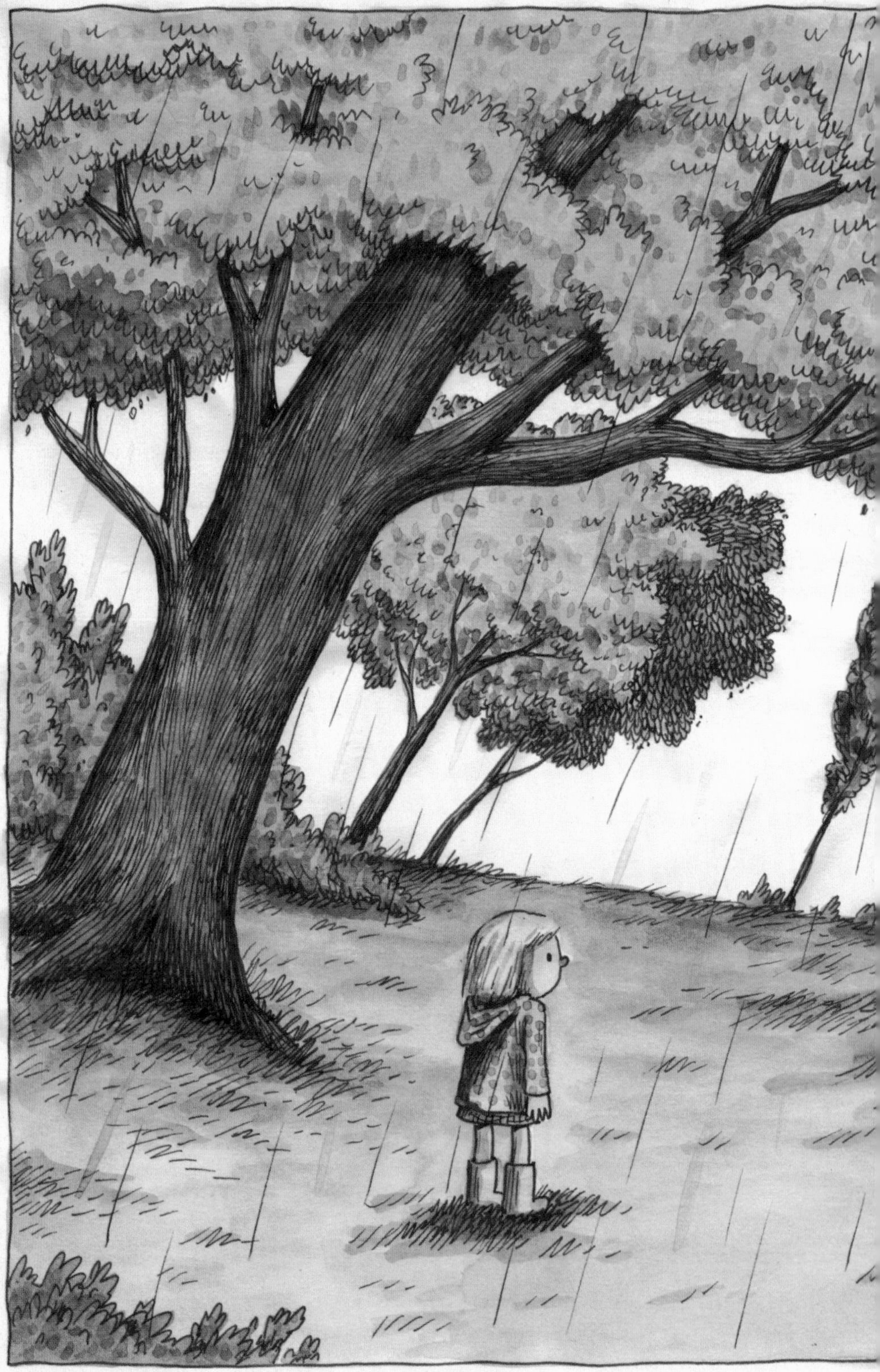

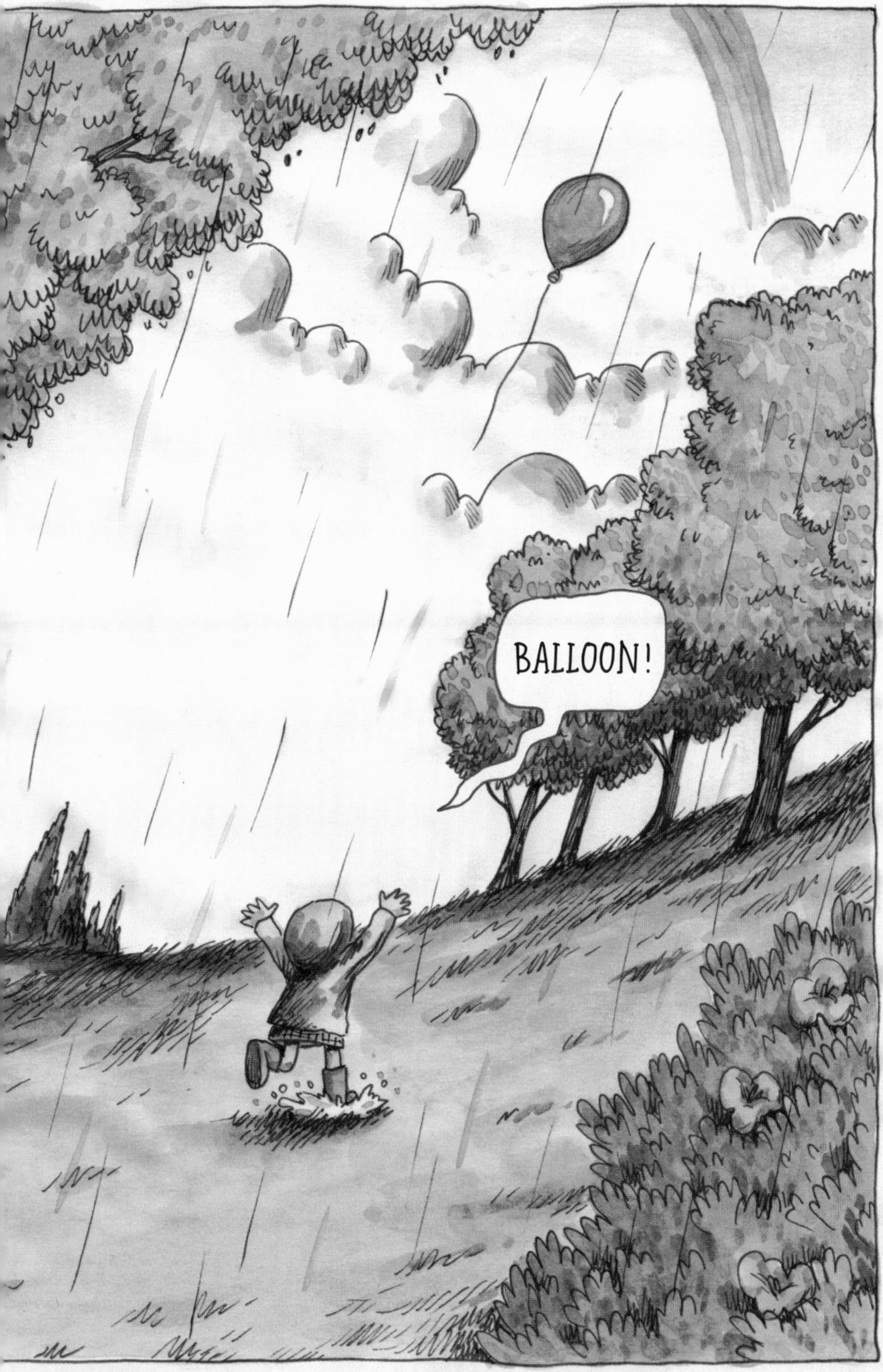
BALLOON!

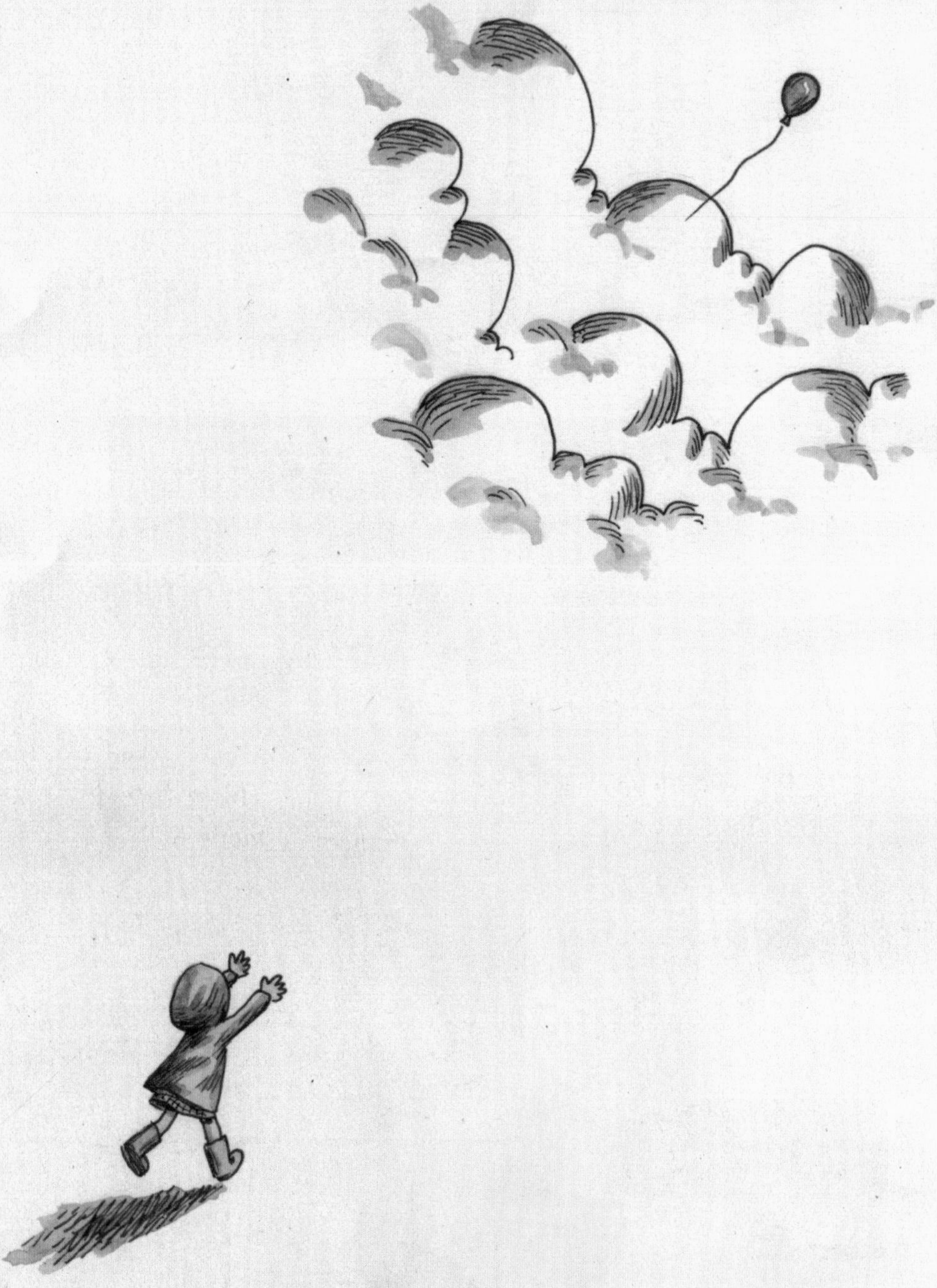

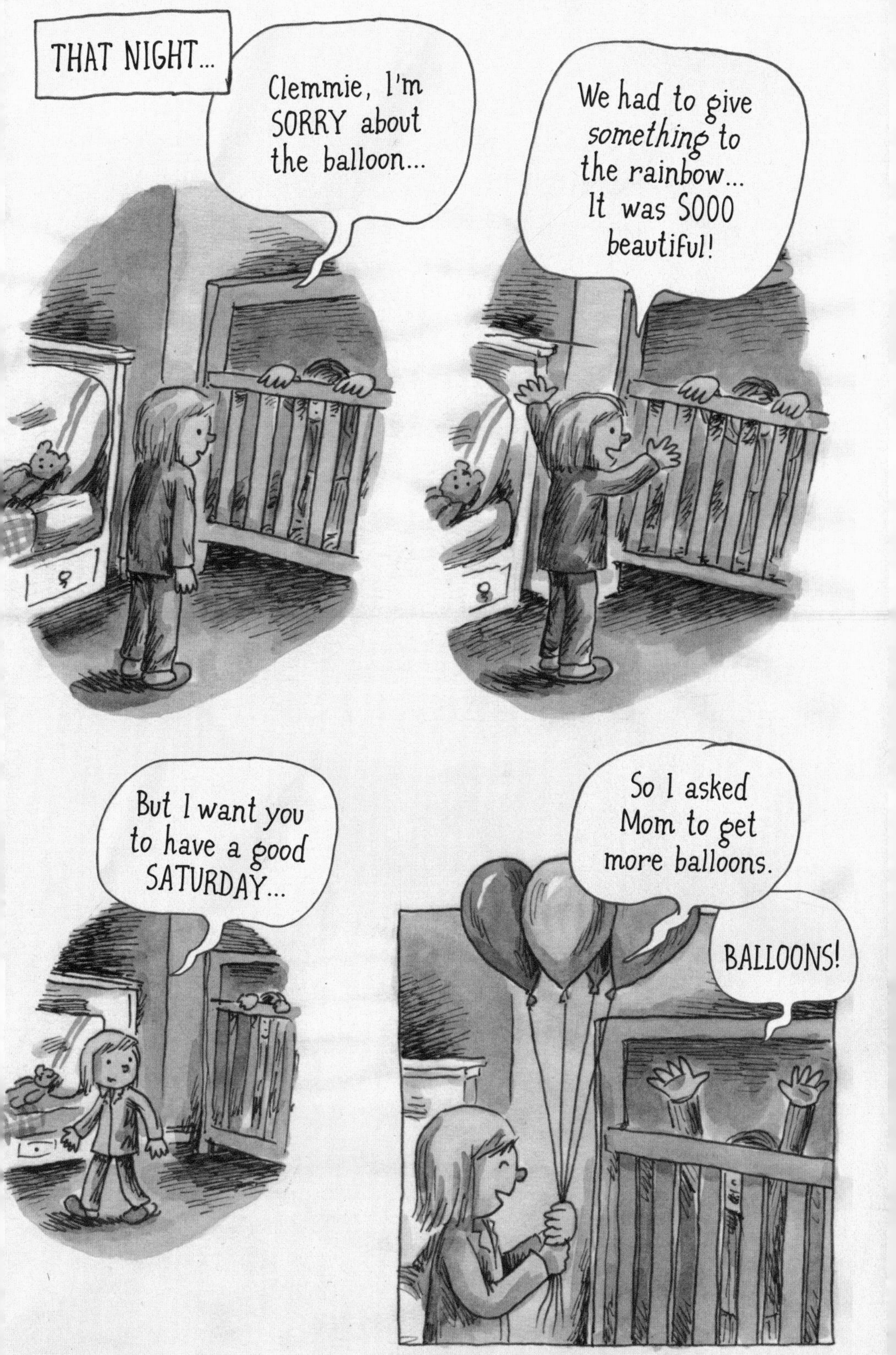
THAT NIGHT...
Clemmie, I'm SORRY about the balloon...
We had to give *something* to the rainbow... It was SOOO beautiful!
But I want you to have a good SATURDAY...
So I asked Mom to get more balloons.
BALLOONS!

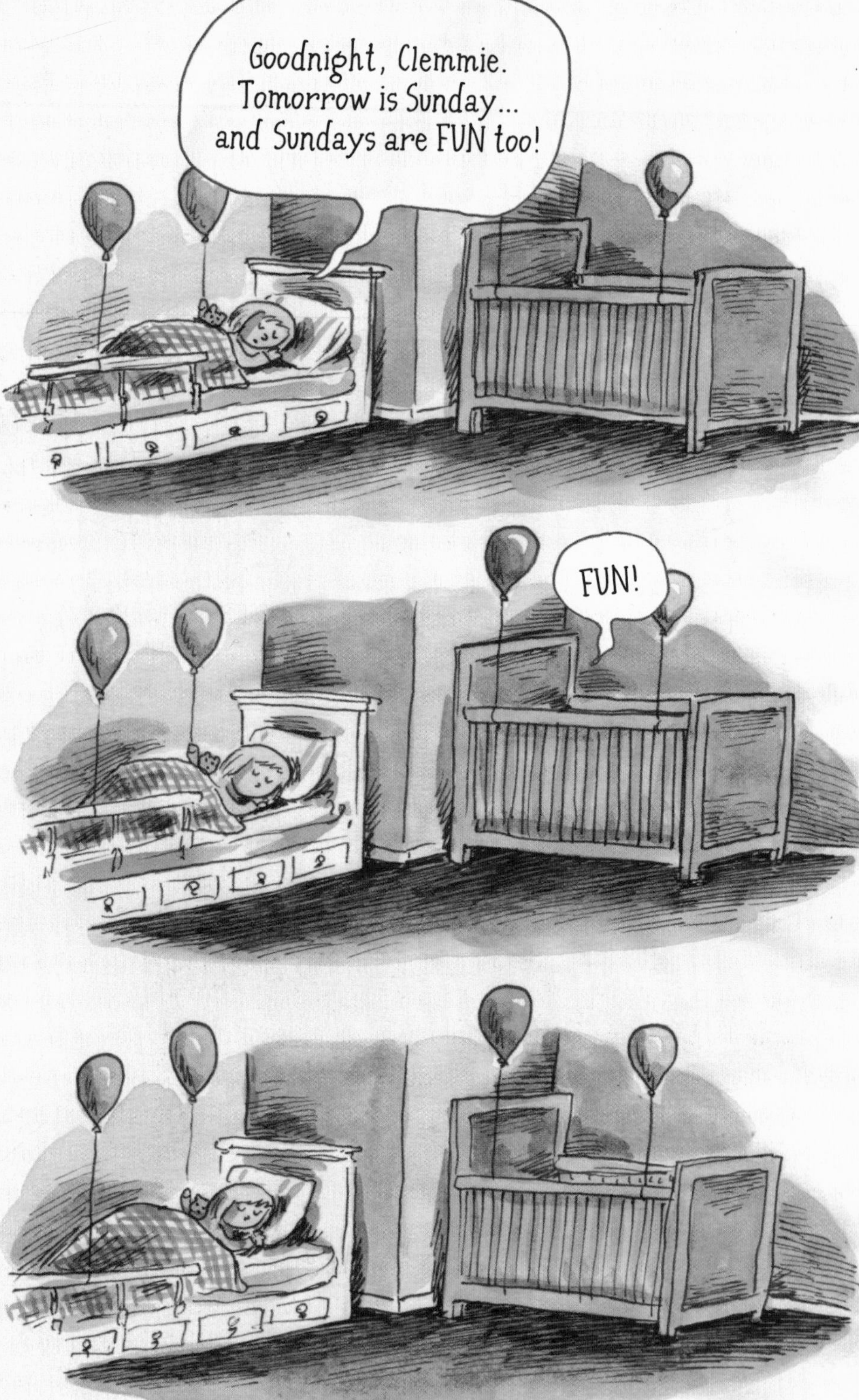
Goodnight, Clemmie.
Tomorrow is Sunday...
...and Sundays are FUN too!
FUN!

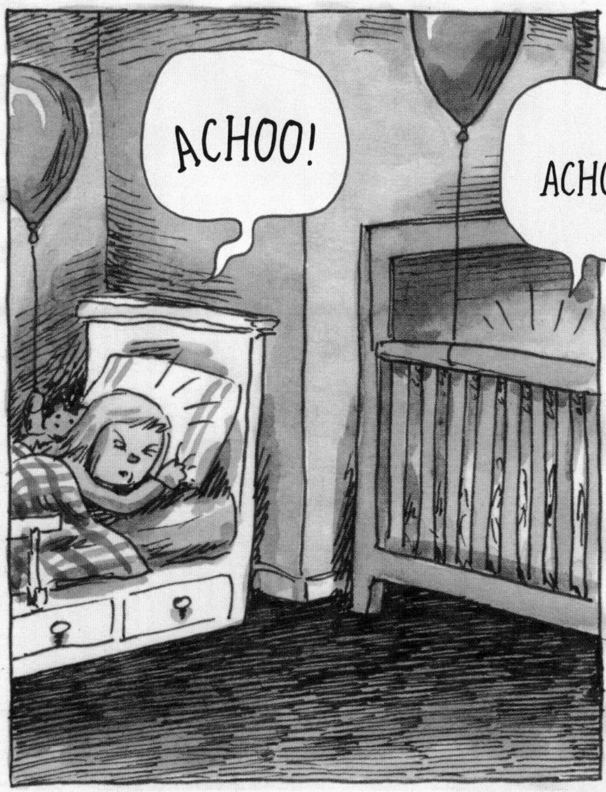
ACHOO!
ACHOO!

THE END

ABOUT THE AUTHOR

RICARDO LINIERS SIRI lives in Buenos Aires with his wife and three daughters: Matilda and Clementina, who inspired this story, and Emma, who was born since. For more than a decade, he has published a popular daily strip, *Macanudo*, in the Argentine newspaper *La Nación*. His work has been published in ten countries from Brazil to the Czech Republic, but this was his first book in the United States. He's now the author of another TOON Book, *Written and Drawn by Henrietta*. Like his daughters, Liniers likes rainy days even more than sunny ones.

—by Matilda, 5

HOW TO READ COMICS WITH KIDS

Kids **love** comics! They are naturally drawn to the details in the pictures, which make them want to read the words. Comics beg for repeated readings and let both emerging and reluctant readers enjoy complex stories with a rich vocabulary. But since comics have their own grammar, here are a few tips for reading them with kids:

GUIDE YOUNG READERS: Use your finger to show your place in the text, but keep it at the bottom of the speaking character so it doesn't hide the very important facial expressions.

HAM IT UP! Think of the comic book story as a play and don't hesitate to read with expression and intonation. Assign parts or get kids to supply the sound effects, a great way to reinforce phonics skills.

LET THEM GUESS. Comics provide lots of context for the words, so emerging readers can make informed guesses. Like jigsaw puzzles, comics ask readers to make connections, so check a young audience's understanding by asking "What's this character thinking?" (but don't be surprised if a kid finds some of the comics' subtle details faster than you).

TALK ABOUT THE PICTURES. Point out how the artist paces the story with pauses (silent panels) or speeded-up action (a burst of short panels). Discuss how the size and shape of the panels carry meaning.

ABOVE ALL, ENJOY! There is of course never one right way to read, so go for the shared pleasure. Once children make the story happen in their imaginations, they have discovered the thrill of reading, and you won't be able to stop them. At that point, just go get them more books, and more comics.

TOON-BOOKS.com

SEE OUR FREE ONLINE CARTOON MAKERS, LESSON PLANS, AND MUCH MORE